THE BETTER BROWN STORIES

ALLAN AHLBERG

The Better Brown Stories

Illustrated by Fritz Wegner

VIKING

VIKING

Published by the Penguin Group
Penguin Books Ltd, 27 Wrights Lane, London W8 5TZ, England
Penguin Books USA Inc., 375 Hudson Street, New York, New York 10014, USA
Penguin Books Australia Ltd, Ringwood, Victoria, Australia
Penguin Books Canada Ltd, 10 Alcorn Avenue, Toronto, Ontario,
Canada M4V 3B2
Penguin Books (NZ) Ltd, 182–190 Wairau Road, Auckland 10, New Zealand

Penguin Books Ltd, Registered Offices: Harmondsworth, Middlesex, England

First published 1995
3 5 7 9 10 8 6 4 2

Consultant Designer: Douglas Martin

Filmset by Goodfellow & Egan, Cambridge

Printed in England by Clays Ltd, St Ives plc

A CIP catalogue record for this book is available from the British Library

ISBN 0–670–85894–3

Contents

Acknowledgements

T HE WRITER wishes to thank his secretary, Anne Boulter, and editor, Philippa Milnes-Smith, for all their help. Also Robert Louis Stevenson, Sir Arthur Conan Doyle, W. Somerset Maugham, Enid Blyton and Raymond Briggs, without whose work this book could not have been written.

1

Hoovering

HERE WE ARE AGAIN in the peaceful and popular little town of Snuggleton-on-Sea. Things haven't changed much since we were here before. Its streets and alleyways, its cobbled lanes and coastal walks are just as they always were. The hotel and the bank, church, fire station and bingo hall, all remain unchanged. Down at the harbour a row of fishing boats bob as always at the quayside. Everywhere, from one end of the town to the other, there is the sound and smell of the sea.

The people, too, are more or less unchanged. The Café Owner is cleaning his outside tables. Paper Boys and Girls, the Postman and the Milkman are out on their regular rounds. The Wet-Fish Man is driving his van down to the harbour. The Vicar is drinking tea, his cat is in the pear tree, some Mysterious Men

coffee actually)

are messing about at the back of the supermarket, and the Runner is getting ready for an early morning jog.

Meanwhile at Number 38 Clifford Avenue we find, as usual, our old friends the Browns . . .

1

It was eight o'clock on a warm May morning. Mr Brown was in the bathroom singing the Hallelujah Chorus. Mrs Brown was in the kitchen mixing home-made muesli and chopping bananas for breakfast. Ten-year-old Betsy was brushing her hair while revising for a French test. Nine-year-old Brian was watching an item on TV about Cruft's Dog Show. Baby Brown was upstairs in his cot.

The family gathered in the kitchen and sat down to breakfast. Mr Brown mentioned a big financial deal he was handling at the bank; he was the Assistant Manager. Betsy spoke enthusiastically of her French test, in which she was expecting to do well. Brian apologized for the state of his room and said he would tidy it up after school. Mrs Brown nodded amiably but otherwise said little. She was looking forward to having the house to herself and getting on with a bit of hoovering.

Silence.   Immobility.   Shock.

'Hang on a minute.' Mrs Brown lowered her spoon. 'What's all this? "Looking forward to a bit of *hoovering*"?' A puzzled frown. 'I hate hoovering.'

'I hate muesli, come to that,' said Mr Brown, staring perplexedly into his bowl.

'Me, too!' cried Brian.

'And I hate French!' Betsy yelled.

Silence . Immobility . Shock

Silence again as the Browns considered their unusual situation.

Mrs Brown said, '*Who writes this rubbish?*'

'The Writer, I suppose,' said Mr Brown. 'The Baker bakes, the Fisherman fishes, the Teacher teaches –'

'More or less,' muttered Betsy.

'– and the Writer writes.'

'Where does he live?'

'One of those seamen's cottages on Slope Street, I believe.'

'Hm.' Mrs Brown rubbed her chin. 'Bit of hoovering . . . Let's go and see him.'

Twenty minutes later the Browns left the house. Brian and Betsy took turns with the pushchair. As they climbed the hill towards Slope Street, they were overtaken by the Runner returning from his run. His heavy breathing made Brian jump.

The Browns were talking non-stop.

3

'And another thing,' said Mr Brown; 'why do we have to have Auntie Marjorie to lunch *every* Sunday?'

'And why is it always vegetable casserole?' cried Betsy. 'And plum pudding?'

'Why is it always me that cooks it?' Mrs Brown added.

'I love plum pudding,' said Brian.

And a little later:

'Why not more variety – less routine?'

'More adventures!'

'Surprises!'

'More pocket-money!'

'Less homework!'

'Less *house*work.'

'*No* housework!'

'. . . More dogs.'

2

The Writer

NUMBER 14 Slope Street was part of a terrace. It had small square windows either side of a lowish door. The door was painted red and had a brass knocker.

Mrs Brown knocked. A hush descended on the entire family. They were beginning to feel embarrassed. There was no answer.

Mrs Brown knocked again.

'Perhaps he's not up yet,' said Mr Brown.

'Well he ought to be – it's nine o'clock.'

'Writers sometimes work till midnight,' said Betsy. 'I read that somewhere.'

'Yes,' said Mrs Brown, 'and a writer wrote it. Let's look round the back.'

But knocking on the back door brought no response either. Peering through the window, the Browns could see a table with the remains of breakfast – toast, boiled egg, coffee cup – spread out upon a blue-and-white cloth.

'No muesli for him,' muttered Mr Brown.

'*And* he's got a dog,' said Brian, spotting a kennel.

A path led down to a remarkably long garden. The

view was tremendous; half the town and the entire curve of the bay were spread out below them. The garden itself was a picture: flowers and bushes, trees and grass. To one side there was a rabbit hutch. A

A Picture

carousel of pegged-out washing fluttered near the house. At the far end, almost invisible in the trees, there was –

'Look, Mum – a shed!' cried Brian.

'Writers work in sheds,' said Betsy; 'sometimes.'

Mrs Brown removed the baby from his pushchair, handed him to her husband and continued down the path. The others followed.

The shed was green. It had a door in the side, a sloping roof and a row of windows at the front, one of which was open.

Mrs Brown looked in. A man was sitting at a desk looking out. He was slightly built, with brown hair, a greying beard and blue eyes. He was wearing a pair of gold-rimmed spectacles – peering over them, in fact – and had a pen in his hand.

'Oh!' cried Mrs Brown.

'Goodness me!' declared the man.

Mrs Brown was first to recover. 'Excuse me, are you the Writer?'

'Er . . . yes,' said the man.

'Well our name's Brown. We'd like a word.'

'You've come to the right place then.' The man smiled. 'There's loads of them here.' He opened the door. 'Did you say "Brown"?'

'Yes,' said Mr Brown, shyly. 'Mr and Mrs.'

'Brian . . .'

'And Betsy!' added the children.

'What – from Clifford Avenue?' The man, the Writer that is, looked confused.

Mrs Brown nodded.

'Good grief! You'd better come in.'

The shed contained, apart from the desk, a typist's chair, an easy chair, some shelves, an electric heater and a tiny table with kettle, cup, sugar bowl and so on laid out on it. There was a rug on the floor and photographs, posters, children's letters, page-proofs and newspaper cuttings on the walls.

Mrs Brown took a seat in the easy chair, with the

baby on her lap. Brian and Betsy occupied the arms of the chair. Mr Brown stood in the doorway.

The Writer swivelled to face them. 'So, here we are. How can I . . .?'

'It's about this story we're in,' said Mrs Brown.

'Oh, yes. What seems to be . . .?'

'It's full of hoovering.'

'And muesli.'

'And French tests!'

'And tidying my room!'

'And another thing!' This was Betsy. 'All our names start with "B". That's just silly.'

'Yes,' said Brian, 'and you're always saying how old we are, like "nine-year-old Brian" and that. And there's no dogs in this story anywhere.'

'As for the bank,' said Mr Brown, mildly, 'it's not the most exciting of places.'

'Nor's the kitchen,' added Mrs Brown, 'in which I

mostly appear to live.' She adjusted the baby on her lap. 'In a nutshell, y'see, the thing about this story is – it's boring.'

The Writer was quite bowled over by this on-slaught. (The word that most upset him, of course, was "boring".) He removed his glasses and gazed out of the window.

'This is a bombshell,' he said.

Then: 'No one's ever complained before.'

And finally: 'I've won prizes.'

The Browns shuffled uncomfortably. Brian began to read one of the posters. The baby hiccuped.

Mr Brown said, 'It's not that we mean to hurt your feelings.'

'It's just a different story,' added Mrs Brown. 'That's all we want.'

'Hm.' The Writer swivelled again to face them. His spirits, it seemed, were lifting. 'A different story . . .' He drummed his fingers on the desk. '*Four* different stories. Hm . . . no muesli.'

Not long after, the Browns left in a hurry. Mr Brown was late for work, the children for school, the baby for his clinic. All the same, Brian found time to visit the rabbits. There were three of them sitting out on a patch of grass next to the hutch.

Back in the shed, the Writer made a cup of tea. He took a pile of paper and dropped it in the waste-paper basket. He stared out at the view. Suddenly, once more a face stared in at him.

'Sorry to bother . . .' It was Mrs Brown again, breathing hard. 'I forgot – there's one more thing.' She opened the door and popped her head in. 'It's hairdressers – perms – I hate 'em.'

'Right,' said the Writer. 'I'll try to remember.'

And Mrs Brown was gone.

The Writer sipped his tea. He watched the neighbour's cat come strolling up the path, listened to the distant surging waves down in the bay. Presently, he reached for a fresh sheet of paper and took up his pen.

3

Milko!

DAWN, though darkness hovers still above the peaceful and popular little town of Snuggleton-on-Sea. Street lamps shine; swirls of mist drift up from the harbour. In the depot of Snuggleton Co-operative Dairies a figure in a white coat stands beside his white electric cart. He has a bottle in his hand, but it contains no ordinary milk.

A liquid: purplish and green, effervescing slightly with green fumes rising. The man, the Milkman, raises the bottle to his lips and drinks.

'Aaargh!' A dreadful echoing groan.

The Milkman staggers, clutching his throat. He hunches forward, shuddering and groaning more. The features of his face, meanwhile, appear to melt and rearrange themselves. Gone the cheery milk-man's smile, and in its place . . .

The Milkman – if still he can be called a milkman – straightens up, observes his own reflection in a driving mirror and grins an evil grin.

'Milko!' he cries – or rather growls, 'Merlkaah!' – and sets off on his round.

It was eight o'clock on a cool May morning. Mr Brown was in the bathroom singing the Toreador Song. Mrs Brown was boiling eggs for breakfast. Betsy was revising for a science test. Brian was reading one of his many dog books.

At twenty to nine Mr Brown set off for the bank and the children left for school. Mrs Brown stood in the doorway waving. Seeing the empty bottles on the step, it occurred to her: 'The Milkman's late.'

Alone in the house, Mrs Brown consulted her list of jobs. She rang her mother, changed the fuse in the plug on Betsy's computer and got out the Hoover. Then, thinking better of it, she made a cup of tea and read the paper.

Meanwhile, out in the street the sound of clinking bottles could be heard. 'Good,' thought Mrs Brown. 'About time, too.'

Her attention had been caught by an article on mountain bikes. (Brian was forever on about them, when he wasn't on about dogs.) From along the street there came a faint scream, which Mrs Brown failed to hear. A dog barked, growled and whimpered. She missed that too. This article was really informative. Footsteps now on the gravel path, and then the doorbell rang.

With the paper still in her hand, Mrs Brown opened the door. A familiar figure was standing there with his back to her.

'Mornin', Gerry – two pints pl . . .'

While slowly he turned.

'Waaarh!' growled the Milkman.

Mrs Brown screamed. Back she staggered and in *he* staggered and slammed the door.

'Gerry?' Mrs Brown retreated. 'This isn't like you.'

The mad and hairy Milkman lumbered forward.

'Let's be reasonable.'

'Waaarh!'

Frantically, Mrs Brown looked round for something to . . . She grabbed a Hoover attachment. 'Keep off!'

But this seemed only to madden him more. 'Har!' he growled, and grabbed the other end. A desperate tug-of-war ensued. The Milkman's strength was monstrous. He pulled the brush end off with ease and kept on coming.

Mrs Brown – 'This is a nightmare!' – stumbled back and tripped over the Hoover cable.

Now the triumphant Milkman loomed above her.

'Oh, no!'

His terrible hairy hands came down.

'Help!'

And grabbed . . . the Hoover.

He took it all: cylinder, attachments, even those complicated bits that nobody ever uses. Mrs Brown was flabbergasted. She scrambled to her feet and made for the kitchen. The Milkman, clutching his prizes, backed off towards the door.

Then the children arrived.

'Hallo, Mum!'

'What's Gerry doing . . . here?'

While slowly, once more, he turned.

The children gasped, the Milkman dropped his curtain attachment and Mrs Brown surprised herself. Snatching the baby's porridge pot from the worktop,

14

she hurtled forward and walloped the back of the Milkman's head.

The insensible Milkman lay on the floor. Mrs Brown and the children rushed to each other's arms.

'Oh, Mum!'

'What's happened?'

Mrs Brown told all she knew, which wasn't much.

Brian said, 'Let's tie him up!'

'No,' said Betsy. 'Phone the police.'

But the phone was too near the Milkman, who was beginning to stir.

'Har!' he groaned, and sat up.

The Browns stood poised in the doorway. Something was happening. A series of dreadful shudders began to rack the Milkman's body. 'Har!' he groaned again, and, 'Aaargh!', and finally, 'Oh!' The features of his face, meanwhile, appeared to melt and re-arrange themselves. Gone the monstrous milkman's grin, and in its place . . .

'Where am I?'

Gerry the Milkman sat in the kitchen drinking a glass of milk, while Mrs Brown bathed the lump on his head. The children crowded in beside him.

Mrs Brown said, 'What beats me is, what made you do it?'

Gerry shook his head and winced. 'I dunno. Must've been that potion I drank.'

'What potion?'

'Don't ask me.' Gerry reached for a biscuit. 'Anyway, somehow I had this irresistible urge to swipe Hoovers.'

Mrs Brown paused in her nursing. 'Hoovers?'

'Yes.' Gerry looked thoroughly ashamed. 'I don't know what came over me.'

'Don't you?' Mrs Brown put down her cotton-wool and bottle of TCP. 'Well, I do.' She addressed the children. 'Get your coats on.'

'What for?'

'Where're we going?'

And Mrs Brown, already in the hall herself, yelled, 'Guess!'

The Writer was in his shed gazing thoughtfully out of the window. The first butterflies of summer were flitting across the garden. There was a smell of wood smoke in the air. From some way off, above the surge of the sea, a car alarm was sounding.

In burst Mrs Brown and the children, with the Milkman, carrying the baby, not far behind.

Mrs Brown wasted no time. 'What d'you mean by it?'

'Hm?' enquired the Writer, mildly.

'Don't give me that. What d'you mean by it? All this nonsense with a monster milkman? Somebody could've got hurt.'

'Somebody did,' said Gerry.

'It wasn't boring, though, was it?' said the Writer.

'Never mind that! Look at this perfectly innocent milkman – look at the lump on his head!'

The Milkman bowed his head, the better to display his injuries.

'My word,' the Writer said, 'you pack a wallop, Mrs Brown.'

'It wasn't *me*!' Mrs Brown paused. 'Not really.'

Then she was off again. 'And another thing! Why aren't these children in school?'

'Burst boiler,' said the Writer, 'flooded classrooms. Didn't they tell you?'

'There was too much going on,' said Brian.

'And *another* thing! This baby!' Mrs Brown grabbed

the baby and held him out. 'I meant to tell you this before. You keep forgetting him. Upstairs in his cot for hours on end – it's shameful.'

'Yes, sorry about that. I'm not so good on babies. Don't know much about them.' The Writer shuffled the papers on his desk. 'There again, it's not all bad. Your hair looks nice.'

'Does it?'

'It's lovely, Mum!' cried Betsy.

'Smashin'!' Gerry said.

'Oh!'

'And not a hairdresser in sight,' the Writer added. 'All natural waves.'

Mrs Brown, despite herself, was smiling. 'Anyway, it's not the Hoover I hate, silly – it's hoovering. We need the Hoover.'

'Let these two do it then,' the Writer said. 'Let *Mr* Brown have a go.'

'That's a thought.' Mrs Brown sighed. 'Anyway, that's it. We want no more of these ridiculous stories.' She gave the baby an absent-minded kiss. 'It's all nonsense.'

Before the Writer could protest, the children beat him to it.

'Oh, Mum!'

'That's not fair!'

'You've had your turn!'

Mrs Brown relented. 'All right, but leave me out of it.'

'And me,' said Gerry.

Mrs Brown, the baby and the Milkman departed. Brian and Betsy stayed on for a while, reminding the Writer of their hopes and preferences, and arguing over who should be next. In the end they tossed for it.

After they'd left, the Writer had some lunch with his mother and took a nap. In the afternoon he returned to the shed. He wrote, DON'T FORGET THE BABY on a piece of card, and pinned it to the wall.

The Writer leaned back in his chair, the pen still in his hand, and gazed at the view. He did this for a considerable time. Then, 'Fog!' he cried, and began to write.

4

Unbelievable Pawprints

IN ONES and twos and sixes, even, the dogs are disappearing. The Mayor has lost a cocker spaniel, the Vicar a Great Dane. The Paper Girl's two mongrel terriers have gone and the Runner's whippet. Also missing are the Wet-Fish Man's Old English Sheepdog, Gerry the Milkman's elderly boxer, the Traffic Warden's entire litter of beautifully marked Jack Russell puppies and many more.

The police are baffled. They used their tracker dog to assist them in the search and he went missing. Following many hours of investigation only three clues have emerged:

(1) Dogs disappear only on foggy nights.

(2) Sometimes their kennels disappear with them.

(3) This clue is considered too disturbing to reveal to the general public; it has to do with certain *unbelievable* pawprints.

Brian Brown, who had no dog of his own, nevertheless knew more about dogs than any boy in Snuggleton. His room was full of dog books; in school even the teacher had come to rely on his superior knowledge. At home Brian did his share of the hoovering and often boiled the eggs for the family breakfast. All he asked for in return was a dog or, more particularly, a puppy. His thoughtless parents, however, refused to consider it, and his apathetic sis-

ter was no help either. Brian endured this situation with dignity. As time went by, he slowly covered the walls of his room with dog pictures, collected cheap sets of dog cigarette cards whenever he went to an antique fair . . . and waited.

It was half-past ten on a cool May night. Curtains were drawn and TVs glowed in Clifford Avenue. At Number 38, Brian was making a cheese and pickled onion sandwich. Earlier that day his parents and his sister Betsy had set off by coach to a hockey tournment in which Betsy was taking part. Now they had broken down on the motorway.

Brian ate his sandwich at the kitchen table and listened to the radio. Suddenly there was a newsflash: 'WE INTERRUPT THIS PROGRAMME TO REPORT ANOTHER MISSING DOG IN SNUGGLETON'. It was the Plumber's Pekinese, apparently. The police were

at the scene of the crime in Roman Road. Owners were again advised to check the whereabouts of their dogs and warned to 'STAY INDOORS'.

Brian wandered over to the window. His cool yet curiously reckless mind was considering this business of the missing dogs. He drew the curtain aside. Fog, drifting in from the sea, pressed up against the glass and smothered the view. The street lamp was barely visible. Brian listened: faint rumblings from the fridge, gurgling water in the radiator. Outside, a distant throbbing. He switched off the light.

The throbbing sound grew louder. Along the street, approaching through the almost solid fog, Brian could discern a pair of headlights. No, they were too high for headlights . . . and too close together. He looked again. Out of the shrouds of fog and into the street lamp's muffled glow, a majestic, enormous and altogether unbelievable dog (with dazzling eyes) was making its way up Clifford Avenue.

Coolly, Brian hid the house key in its usual place; recklessly, he pursued the dog. His brain was buzzing. The biggest dog known to man (and Brian) was listed in the *Guinness Book of Records*: Zorba, an Old English Mastiff. It was almost a metre high at the shoulder and weighed 155.58 kg. 'Well,' thought Brian, 'this one's bigger.'

He had another thought too.

In Greengate Road, he caught a glimpse of the dog as it passed a petrol station. The attendant glimpsed it too, and ran off. An unsteady man came out of a pub, spotted the dog and went back in. Brian, impelled as though by some mysterious force, stuck to the trail. Through fog-bound and otherwise deserted streets, he followed the huge unearthly creature.

They were approaching the harbour where, if anything, the fog was thicker. There was a ramp. A section of the road sloped sharply down into . . . a cavern. The giant dog descended. There was a barrier – Brian knew where he was! The underground car park, opened mainly for the holiday season; closed the rest of the year. Closed now.

Brian crouched beside a litter bin. As the barrier went up, he heard, or thought he heard, a mournful howl. It appeared to come from the gigantic dog. Brian broke into a sweat as instantly, with his expert ear, he recognized the sound. It was a Pekinese.

The dog descended into the depths of the car park. Brian followed. A faint chorus of barking began to be heard. Eventually, the dog left the ramp and advanced into the centre of a shadowy, ill-lit space. Brian crept in behind a pillar. The barking was coming from scores of dogs in crates. As the giant dog emerged, it ceased.

On the far side, a furniture van was parked. A couple of Mysterious Men were loading something into it. They left the van and approached the dog. The crates of kidnapped dogs were arranged in a row along one wall with a number of kennels nearby. There was a tremendous aroma of Pedigree Chum.

Brian saved his attention for the giant dog. Despite the gloom, this was the best view he'd had. He tried to guess its size (it was higher than the van!) and weight – a ton, perhaps. He wondered about its origin and diet.

Suddenly, a whirring noise. The dog's eyes grew dim, a *trapdoor* opened in its belly and a set of steps

24

descended to the ground. Presently, a Pekinese and three or four other dogs came trotting out. The Mysterious Men grabbed them and shoved them into a crate. And then a small Mysterious Man came jauntily down the steps, and lit a cigarette.

The Mysterious Men were huddled together. Brian heard snatches of conversation.

'Only five!'

'Wolverhampton Wanderers . . .'

(it sounded like).

'Gerra move on.'

His thoughts in turmoil, Brian crept from behind the pillar. The Mysterious Men were bustling back and forth, carrying mysterious objects. He began to consider his options. The cool option was to watch and wait, gather evidence, get the number of the van. The sensible option, find a phone-box, 999. The reckless option . . .

The Really Sensible Option

Brian had edged his way round to the far wall. A spaniel in a crate was whimpering at him. Reaching in to pat the dog's head, Brian received a joyful lick. Then a *fourth* Mysterious Man grabbed him.

'Waarish?'

Brian kicked and yelled. The other men came running. He kicked again, connected with a mysterious shin and struggled free. He ran to the ramp. But the littlest man beat him to it. He ran to the van, but a fifth Mysterious Man rose up to block his way. Outnumbered, surrounded, with nowhere else to go, Brian raced full tilt up the extended flight of steps and *into* the enormous dog.

Brian remained calm. He found a lever which retracted the steps and closed the trapdoor. More steps led up into the dog's head. Here he discovered a small, cramped area like the cockpit of a plane, with dials, knobs, video screens and a joystick. Brian was good with a joystick – at least, with Betsy's computer he was. He sat at the controls.

The large Mysterious Men were attending to the small one who had tumbled from the steps. The tallest of them started banging on the trapdoor. A ladder was fetched and propped against the side of the dog. Muttered conversations were held.

Meanwhile, back in the dog twiddling knobs, Brian had inadvertently sent a fax and made himself a cup of coffee. Gradually, though, he was getting the hang of things.

A familiar throbbing.

'Warrat?' cried one of the men.

Glowing eyes and a clattering ladder.

'Woot!' yelled another.

The gigantic dog was on the move!

The Mysterious Men ran. Clumsily at first, but with increasing skill, the dog pursued them. Brian was having the time of his life! He could observe the men on the video screens and follow them with the joystick. There were other controls, too: water cannon, for instance.

Tremendous confusion: colliding Mysterious Men – shouts and groans – crushed crates – liberated dogs – howling and barking – fused lights – wildly swinging torch beams. Then, to top it all, just audible above the din, a police siren.

That did it.

The Mysterious
Men fled.

No, not yet!

Yes. The
Mysterious
Men . . .

Let 'em stay!

No . . . fled.

Bruised, soaked and bewildered, they leapt into the van and headed up the ramp. The barrier was down; the Mysterious Men smashed through it. The fog was thicker than ever; the Mysterious Men drove madly into it. The *police* were in attendance; the Mysterious Men sped past them and, with a screech of brakes . . . disappeared.

Moments later, the enormous dog emerged from the depths of the car park, and Brian emerged from the depths of the dog. The police were dumbstruck.

A policewoman gathered her wits first. 'Are you the boy who phoned?'

'Yes,' said Brian. (There was a phone in the dog.)

'Concerning the case of the missing dogs?'

'Yes,' said Brian. 'They're down here – come and see!'

An anxious-looking constable took Brian's arm. 'Was there a tracker dog among them?'

'Yes!'

The Constable beamed and clapped his hands. 'Oh, good!'

Fog swirled as ever, it seemed, along the seafront. The unattended giant dog stood like a Trojan horse at the car-park entrance. Silence, except for the sea

Is that it?

and a far-off foghorn. Then, a whirring noise; the folding steps went folding upwards, the trapdoor closed. A throbbing sound; an almost imperceptible shift of gears. The dog was on the move *again*. By the time the police recollected their duty and hurried back, there was nothing to see. Except, that is, for a couple of unbelievable pawprints.

When Brian arrived home at half-past midnight, he met his startled family on the doorstep just arriving themselves. (The baby, I should have mentioned this earlier, was at his Grandma's.)

Over a cup of tea, the Constable gave details of Brian's remarkable deeds. So did Brian.

Forgot him again!

'This is a rare boy,' said the Constable. 'However . . . ' He went on to suggest that perhaps it wasn't all that wise of Mr and Mrs Brown to have left him alone in the house. 'Capable though he is.'

'You're right, of course.' Mr Brown looked chastened. 'I must say it surprised *me*. We've never done it before.'

Mrs Brown said nothing, but bit her lip and cuddled her hero son.

The next morning, as you can imagine, the Browns had trouble getting up. Everyone was rushing around. At 8.15 Grandma Weaver arrived with the baby, and left in a hurry. The children ate their boiled eggs while listening to the radio, which was all about Brian.

The doorbell rang. Brian and Betsy heard voices in the hall. Presently, Mr Brown entered the kitchen carrying a cardboard box. 'For you,' he said to Brian, placing it on the table. 'From a grateful owner.'

Brian dropped his spoon and lifted the lid.

It had a puppy in it . . . of course.

5

Messages

LATER THAT DAY, after finishing work at the bank, Mr Brown called in to see the Writer. He, as it happened, was going out to the pub.

'Join me,' he said, as he waved to his mum. 'It's only round the corner.'

'Well, er . . .' This wasn't quite what Mr Brown had had in mind.

'Go on, just a quick one.'

The pub was The Baskerville Hound in Dove Street; low ceiling, genuine beams and at that time of day more or less deserted.

'Pint, George,' said the Writer as he stood at the bar. And to Mr Brown, 'What'll you have?'

'Er – half a shandy.'

'Have a pint,' said the Writer.

Mr Brown sighed. 'All right then.'

They carried their pints to a table and sat down.

'So what can I do for you? I was half expecting Brian.'

'Clarinet lesson,' said Mr Brown.

'Oh yes, I forgot.'

Mr Brown fumbled in his pockets. 'The thing is, I'm here as a sort of . . . messenger.' He produced a small blue notebook.

'I've got one of those,' said the Writer.

Mr Brown took a swig and consulted his notes. 'Brian's pleased – well, ecstatic, actually. It was brilliant, he says, especially the puppy. He's curious, though, about that mechanical dog.'

'Oh yes?'

'Wants to know, let's see . . . what kind of motor it had, and where it's gone.'

'The motor's electrical,' said the Writer, 'probably. I'm not so good on motors. As for where it's gone; at this particular moment his guess is as good as mine.'

'Rumour is, it belonged to a Spanish film company.'

The Writer nodded. 'Sounds plausible.'

'Mrs Brown says: about the real dog, did it *have* to be a puppy? It's chewing everything. But she's most concerned – well, both of us, really – about Brian. Left on his own – late at night – riding round in a dog. The police complained, y'know.'

'I know.' The Writer drained his glass. 'Drink up, we'll have another.'

Over the second pint and a bag of smoky bacon crisps, Mr Brown continued. 'Anyway, Mrs Brown says: No more – stop now – it's too risky. On the other hand, of course, Betsy wants *her* story.'

'And you yours,' said the Writer.

Mr Brown ducked his head, shyly. 'Oh no – don't bother about me.'

Over the third pint and a plate of scampi and chips, Mr Brown became quite chatty. 'My wife's a good woman,' he informed the Writer. 'My kids the best. My . . .' He sighed and ate a chip. 'I'm stifled, though, stuck in that bank.'

'I worked in a bank once,' the Writer said. 'Boring.'

'You're right,' said Mr Brown, mournfully. 'A right Writer.'

'What would you do then, if you could?'

'Ah!' Mr Brown gestured with his fork. 'Tell y'a secret: always wanted to be a painter. Run off to Paris – the South Seas – that sort of thing. Make a good story.'

'Somebody already wrote it,' said the Writer. 'Somerset Maugham.'

'Ah.' Mr Brown consumed another chip. 'Just my luck.'

It was late. Mr Brown had meandered home on foot, leaving his car parked in the street. At Number 14, the Writer was having cocoa with his mother and watching TV. Presently, he felt in his pocket and

took out a small blue notebook. From another
pocket he produced a stub of pencil. He gazed for a
while at the wall in front of him, sucked his bit of
pencil briefly and began to write.

6

The Robin Hood Bank

HERE WE ARE once more in the peaceful – well, fairly peaceful – and popular little town of Snuggleton-on-Sea. Things haven't changed much since . . . come to think of it, maybe they have, just a little. The Café Owner, for instance, now has a window-box at the upstairs room of his café. The Wet-Fish Man has a mobile phone and so does the Milkman. The Vicar's cat – a fluffy ginger Persian named Trixie – has, most recently of all, had kittens. There is an American football pitch marked out on the Co-op sportsfield.

It was a quarter to eight on a wet and windy May morning. The fog of previous nights had been blown away. High seas were pounding the harbour. Elsewhere, the Bank Manager was down at the station waiting for the 7.50. The Lollipop Lady, at home in her bungalow on Ocean Road, was gazing in 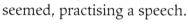 horror and for the umpteenth time at her overdue gas bill. The Mayor was shaving while, rather riskily it seemed, practising a speech.

Meanwhile, at Number 38 . . .

Mr Brown was in the bathroom not shaving or singing either, but hiding. His woes were numerous. Too many pints the previous evening had left him with a headache. This morning he faced a long wet walk to his car. His usually amiable wife was unsympathetic. Their usually tranquil baby had had them up three times in the night. In the kitchen, the puppy had made a mess, chewed a teacosy to shreds and was yapping its head off. On the landing, Brian and Betsy were arguing at the tops of their voices.

Breakfast: Brian and Betsy – still arguing; baby – still howling; puppy – still yapping.

'I'm gonna call him . . . Bobby!' cried Brian, 'Or Bingo, maybe.'

'Waaa!' yelled the baby.

'B's again!' cried Betsy. 'What d'you think, Dad?'

'Balthazar,' said Mr Brown, glumly. 'Beelzebub.'

'Yap, yap!'

'Waaa!'

'Bathsheba.'

'That's a girl's name!'

Mr Brown finished his cup of tea and stood up.

'Got it!' cried Brian, 'Tommy!'

'Waaa!'

'That's no good,' said Mrs Brown. 'What would Uncle Tommy say?'

'Timmy, then.'

'Trapped,' thought Mr Brown, as he reached for his briefcase. 'Bedlam one end – boredom the other.'

'Waaaaa!'

Mr Brown began giving the bank's money away at half-past ten. It happened like this. Old Mrs Rutter, the Lollipop Lady, came in, upset and tearful, hoping to make a small withdrawal with which to pay her gas bill.

'It's fifty pounds I need.'

But there was only twenty in Mrs Rutter's account.

Mr Brown was about to express the usual polite regrets when, as he later explained, 'Something came over me.' Whereupon, he handed Mrs Rutter five new ten-pound notes, and a tissue too. Suddenly, the bank felt just that bit *less* boring.

Subsequently, as other customers arrived, and depending on their circumstances, Mr Brown gave *them* money. In the case of a couple of rich customers, however, he refused them.

Mr Brown was running the bank on his own. The Manager was away on a course and the Assistant Cashier was too preoccupied with thoughts of his own forthcoming marriage to notice anything. The Chief

Cashier was off with a sore throat.

Meanwhile, the word was spreading. A queue had formed at Mr Brown's window and the bank's funds were flowing away. Mr Brown worked through his lunch hour. His face was flushed, his eyes sparkled. By the middle of the afternoon, he had given away £5,486.50.

cricket match actually!

Chief Cashier

At this point the Manager, Mr Smout, arrived in a taxi. 'What *is* going on, Mr Brown? I hear from a reliable source' (one of the rich customers) 'that you are refusing to pay out!'

'Er . . . not exactly,' said Mr Brown.

Then the Manager read the balance sheet and fainted. When he came round, he asked more questions, but mostly answered them himself. 'Who did you think you were – Robin Hood? What did you think you were playing at – Monopoly?'

Finally, his hair awry, his tie twisted, Mr Smout cried out, 'You're fired, of course!', and got on the phone to head office.

Mr Brown returned to *his* office, swept the contents of his desk into the waste-paper basket and tossed his briefcase in on top. Then out he stepped into the dazzling afternoon sunshine.

Mr Brown walked purposefully down Ocean Road. Passers-by greeted him warmly. Motorists wound down their windows to wish him well. Mrs Rutter – on duty at the school crossing – stopped the traffic for him. In Fish Street Mr Brown entered the Moon and Sixpence Café and ordered a cheese and pickled onion sandwich, a slice of Bakewell tart and a cup of tea. Later, on his way to the car park, he called at some other places. One was Gerald Gadsby's: Picture Framers and Artists' Suppliers; and another, Porter-Robinson Ltd: Theatre Tickets, Bureau de Change and Travel Agent.

When Mr Brown arrived home with no briefcase, no tie, a portable easel, set of brushes and box of paints, plus a one-way ticket to Paris, Mrs Brown knew something was up.

'It's now or never, Barbara.' Mr Brown had started packing. 'I've burned my boats at the bank. I want to paint.'

'Why Paris, though?'

'It's the place to go – pass me those socks.'

'But, Bernard, you're nearly forty.'

'All the more reason to make a start.' Mr Brown sighed and folded his cardigan.

When the children arrived home, they were full of rumours about free money. Was it true the bank had been giving it away? Why hadn't they had any? Soon, however, they sensed something was going on. A tie-less dad, distraught mum, suitcase on the bed, ferry-boat ticket and French francs on the sideboard were clues enough.

Their reaction then was swift.

'Oh, Dad!'

'You promised we'd go to CenterParcs!'

'What about the car-boot sale?'

'You'll miss my birthday!' (Betsy's, in three days' time.)

Mr Brown, who was checking his passport, looked ill-at-ease. 'You'll understand when you're older.'

'How about Mum?' said the children. 'Will she understand when she's older?'

'Your mother understands now.'

'No, she doesn't,' said Mrs Brown.

That night, unable to sleep, Betsy crept into Brian's room and woke him up.

'I was having a dream about Dad,' said Brian. 'He

was up on the school roof throwing money away.'

'He'll be gone in the morning,' said Betsy.

'Then that enormous dog showed up and –'

'We might never *see* him again.'

'He'll come back.'

'He might not. I heard them saying something about the *South Seas*.'

Now Mrs Brown, with tousled but still attractively waved hair, appeared in the doorway.

'Betsy, go to bed.'

'I was having a dream about Mum, Dad – I mean Dad, Mum,' said Brian.

Mrs Brown tucked him in and stroked his forehead.

Down in the kitchen, a little dozy yap. Curled up in his basket, Timmy, the puppy, shivered and twitched. The giant dog was in his dreams as well.

It was ten past eight on a warm May morning. Mr Brown was getting ready to leave while everything and everybody was conspiring to make him stay. The children were on their best behaviour and the puppy had used his litter tray. Mrs Brown, though subdued, looked ravishing in a green print dress. Sunlight was streaming in at the kitchen window, birds were chirruping in the guttering and Mr Brown's boiled egg and lightly buttered fingers of toast were simply perfect.

But all to no avail.

The doorbell rang. Taxi.

The children panicked.

'Don't go, Dad!'

'You can paint in my room!'

'I'll get a paper round!'

Mr Brown grasped his suitcase. Mrs Brown stood irresolutely by.

The doorbell again.

'Don't go!'

'Don't go!'

Kisses – cuddles – tears.

'Don't go!'

It was later that morning. Mr Brown stood at the rail of the Snuggleton-to-Calais ferry. Sunlight glittered on the water below. Gulls screeched and circled overhead. Dockers and seamen yelled to each other from ship to shore. Along the quay a fishing boat was unloading its catch; already the Wet-Fish Man was waiting. Elsewhere, the Mayor was making his speech (to the Snuggleton Chamber of Commerce) and the police, baffled again, were attempting to solve the mystery of the *un*robbed bank. They'd heard rumours too, but on making enquiries had been informed that it was purely an internal matter. (Banks tend to hush things up when employees go on the rampage. It's bad for business.)

Meanwhile, the unrobber himself, in his new white suit and Panama hat, remained at the rail. Other passengers, including a party of schoolchildren, were crammed in beside him. A crowd stood at the quayside waving.

Mr Brown gazed down at the array of upturned faces: men and women, boys and girls, babies, dogs, a puppy . . . No, *the* puppy.

Yes, there he was, tugging on the end of a lead which Brian was holding. And there was Betsy, hang-

ing on to her mother's arm; and there, in his push-chair, was the baby.

Urgent activity now on the quayside: last warnings given – gangways withdrawn – ropes cast off.

The ferryboat was pulling away; Paris beckoned. Mr Brown gripped the rail. In that bright morning light, with more light still bouncing up from the sea, the well-loved faces of his family were startlingly clear. Mrs Brown had her hand up shielding her eyes from the sun. Betsy was sobbing. Brian, hampered by Timmy, was trying vainly to direct the baby's attention towards their departing father.

Suddenly, Mr Brown's heart leapt up inside him. The baby's fluttering podgy hands and Barbara's frown were just too much. He sprang to the rail, tossed aside his hat, kicked off his shoes, drew in the deepest breath of his life . . . and dived.

The children saw it: their father poised and teetering on the rail, his flying hat and unexpectedly elegant dive. The crowd gasped. Mr Brown came bobbing to the surface and struck out for the shore. The crowd cheered.

Mrs Brown scooped up the baby. As Mr Brown came dripping up

the stone steps of the quayside, she rushed into his arms, and he to hers, with the flummoxed baby sandwiched in between. Then Brian and Betsy came hurtling in to form one sobbing, smiling, soaking scrum of family affection. Mr Brown aimed a kiss at the baby's cheek and landed it in his little ear. The puppy was leaping and yapping around them; the crowd, nosy and amused.

Now Mr Brown's sense of relief and joy was gathered up in one intensifying hug.

Betsy protested, 'Help – I'm being crushed!'

'A gorilla has got us!' Mrs Brown declared.

Brian hauled Timmy in to join the fun.

The baby . . . burped.

7

Nothing Happening

A CLINK of bottles, crunch of gravel, ring of bell.
'Mornin', Mrs B!'

'Mornin', Gerry – two pints please.'

'Two pints it is,' says Gerry. 'Heard the news?'

'What news?'

'Some Mysterious Men,' says Gerry. 'Four of 'em,
or was it five? Anyway, the police have got 'em.'

'Really?'

'Yeah. Messin' about on the church roof, they
were. Or was it the town hall?'

It was twenty past ten on a sunny May morning at
Snuggleton Primary. Betsy Brown and her friend
Charlotte Spooner were struggling with an English
assignment.

'How d'you spell "dictionary"?'

Betsy, in particular, had trouble concentrating.
Something, she felt, should somehow be *happening* –
and it wasn't. Also, it was her birthday soon and
thoughts of presents, party and so on crowded her
mind. A further distraction was Kevin Barraclough.
He had been drawing himself to her attention, in

hopes, it seemed, of a last-minute invitation.

'Ask him,' said Charlotte.

'No,' Betsy said. 'We don't want boys.'

After school, the girls went round to the Writer's house. The door was opened by an elderly lady. A smell of baking wafted in the air around her.

'I'm Betsy Brown,' said Betsy.

'I know,' the lady said. 'Heard all about you from my talented son. He's not here, by the way.'

'Oh!'

'No – gone to the London Book Fair, he has. Back tomorrow.'

Betsy's face showed disappointment.

'Wait a minute, though.' The Writer's Mother went back into the house.

All Dark and Delicious

Betsy peered in after her. There was a table with a phone on it; a mirror on the wall with bevelled edges and a painted bluebird.

'We've got one like that,' whispered Betsy. 'Identical.'

The Writer's Mother returned with a plate of jam tarts; strawberry jam, all dark and delicious from the baking.

'Help yourself, dear – and your friend. Have a couple!'

Betsy ate her tarts with relish, though her grumpiness remained. 'A fair,' she thought. 'He's got no business going to a fair. He should be working.'

The next day Betsy returned to the Writer's house with Brian and the baby. The Writer himself opened the door.

'Hallo, there – come on in.'

Brian and Betsy manoeuvred the pushchair into the sitting-room.

Brian said, 'Did y'have fun at the fair?'

'Not really.' The Writer smiled. 'It's only books, y'know, not coconut shies.' He crossed his legs and scratched his ankle. 'Any messages?'

'Yes,' said Brian. 'Three – all from Mum. First, there's too many cheese and pickled onion sandwiches, she says. I like 'em, though.'

'Me too,' said the Writer.

'Too much bawling from the baby.'

The Writer observed the tranquil baby. 'Seems quiet enough.'

'You keep going to extremes, Mum says. All she wants is an average baby. A real one.'

'Right. What's the other thing?'

'Er, let's think. Oh, yes – a job for Dad.'

'I'm working on it,' the Writer said.

Betsy, meanwhile, was working on something too:

her scowl. Now, as direct as ever her mother was, she addressed the Writer. 'What about *my* turn?'

'We're coming to it.'

'Yes, but when? Nothing's happening.'

'We've had to wait,' the Writer said. 'I've been busy. Besides, it's a birthday story.'

'So it's tomorrow then!' cried Brian.

'Yes.' The Writer rubbed his hands. 'She'll have a whale of a time: presents – party. Wish I was eleven.'

'That's the trouble, though,' said Betsy, scowling still. 'I've been thinking: I don't want to be eleven.'

'Really?'

'No. I want to be *thirteen*.'

At that moment the Writer's Mother appeared with a plate of lemon-curd tarts and the evening paper.

Betsy's eyes lit up. 'Lemon curd – my favourite!'

'His too,' said his mother.

The Writer, however, made no response. 'Thirteen,' he said to himself. 'Hm.' He glanced at the paper. 'Goodness, listen to this: "MYSTERIOUS MEN IN CUSTODY".'

'Heard about it,' said Betsy.

'"An indeterminate number of Mysterious Men is rumoured to be in police custody, following a tip-off." There's a photograph too.'

'Let's see,' said Brian. 'I might recognize 'em.'

'Doubt it. They're under a blanket.'

Betsy said, 'There's another thing: names.'

'Oh yes?'

'I'm fed up with "Betsy".'

'What's wrong with it? My mum's named Betsy.'

'That's the trouble, it's too old-fashioned.'

The Writer sighed. 'All right, what do you fancy? Brenda? Belinda?'

'Gazza!' cried Brian.

Betsy stood up and approached the Writer. 'I'll whisper,' she said.

8

Nicola

T EN TO THREE – a hot May afternoon – Clifford
Avenue. In the kitchen of Number 38 Mr and
Mrs Brown were putting the finishing touches to a
superb birthday spread, the centrepiece of which was
a magnificent cake ... with thirteen candles on it.
Upstairs in her room, their daughter Nicola was
putting the finishing touches to her appearance. Having settled which leggings, trainers and vastly baggy
T-shirt to wear, her remaining problem was, which
earrings.

'Try the frogs again,' said Charlotte, lolling back
on the bed.

'Nicola!' Mrs Brown, yelling from the stairs. 'Turn
that racket down!'

Languidly, Nicola leant forward and made a micro-
scopic adjustment to the volume control of her tape
deck.

'Try the fluorescent hoops,' said Charlotte.

Just after three, the doorbell rang. Nicola and Charlotte
thundered down. On the doorstep were a couple of
hefty teenage boys, one of whom in black T-shirt and

torn-at-the-knee jeans seemed vaguely familiar.

'Hi, Nicky – happy birthday!' he said, planting a considerable kiss right on her mouth.

'Hey!' Nicola blushed hugely and pushed him away. 'Who d'you think you are?'

'What's up?' The boy looked startled too. 'It's me – Kevin!'

'Kevin?' Nicola now was doubly horrified. 'Kevin *Barraclough*?'

'Yeah! Stop foolin' around – lerrus in.'

Charlotte, a little behind Nicola, was spluttering with laughter. 'I've got it – he's your boyfriend.'

'No, he's not.'

'Yes, he is,' said the other somewhat plumper boy (with glasses too).

'See!' cried Charlotte, spluttering still.

The other boy smiled shyly. 'And I'm yours.'

The Writer was in his shed staring out of the window, pen in hand. The sun was shining but with a curious green tinge; the sky, though mainly blue, was mauve and almost purple in places. Butterflies hovered over the laburnum bushes. An unlucky bee thumped against the glass.

Then Nicola and Charlotte arrived. On her previous visit, you may recall, Nicola had been decidedly bad-tempered. Now she was furious. 'There you are!'

'Come on in,' said the Writer (unnecessarily).

'First you leave me till last –'

'First . . . last,' murmured the Writer.

'Then nothing happens for ages. Then *kisses* – from Kevin Barraclough! B's again.'

'Thought you'd appreciate a bit of romance at your age. I was kissing girls when I was thirteen.'

'Yes, but did they want you to?'

'They were queuing up.' The Writer smiled.

'It's not funny.' Nicola glared. 'The thing is . . . I'm too young.'

'Juliet was only thirteen,' declared the Writer.

'That's got nothing to do with it.' Nicola flounced into the easy chair. 'Anyway, I'm just gonna sit here and *not budge*. I'm kissing nobody.'

'You can't do that – it's mutiny.'

'So it is.'

'You'll ruin everything,' the Writer said. 'I need those boys.'

'Well, we don't – do we, Char?'

'No,' said Charlotte.

Silence. Faint sounds of traffic in the street. The distant pounding sea.

'Hm.' The Writer twiddled his pen. 'We're stuck then. If you stop there,' he began to imitate a slowing down tape-recorder, 'everything grinds to   a   h a l t.'

Nicola remained unmoved, in both senses.

'No thing   hap   pen   s.'

Total silence.   Immobility.   Blankness.

At this point the Paper Girl arrived, sauntering down the path with a bag over her shoulder and an envelope in her hand.

She stood in the doorway.

'You the Writer?'

The Writer nodded.

'Man asked me to give you this.'

She held out the envelope.

'What man?'

'Dunno.'

'What did he look like?'

'Can't say. He had a balaclava on.'

'In this weather?'

'Yeah.' The Paper Girl turned to leave. 'And sunglasses.'

The Writer studied the envelope front and back, but it was blank. He opened it. 'Oh, no!'

'What's the matter?' cried the girls.

'Listen to this:

"Dear Sir,

YOU WILL WRITE US THE PERFECT CRIME.
YOU WILL WRITE US THE PERFECT ALIBI. YOU
WILL WRITE US THE PERFECT GETAWAY.
OR ELSE.

  The Mysterious Men

P.S. Be advised:
WE HAVE GOT YOUR OLD MUM.'"

'Let's see!' Nicola took the note from the Writer's shaking hand, with Charlotte craning over her shoulder. '"The Mysterious Men" . . . Hang on, I thought the police had got 'em.'

'So they had,' said the Writer, miserably. 'Two years ago.'

Charlotte reached for the note. 'Hey, there's more on the back. "P.P.S. DON'T TRY TO FIND US. NO TRICKS – NO COPS – NO TIP-OFFS."'

Nicola said, 'I get it – *everybody's* two years older.'

The Writer said nothing, too bewildered, it seemed, by the tangled web in which he found himself. Whereupon a large dog came bounding down the garden and threw itself into the shed.

'Timmy?' cried Nicola, beating off the dog's attentions.

And Timmy it was, closely followed by Brian and *his* friend.

What happened next was more confusion: children yelling, dog barking, Writer calling ineffectually for order.

Brian had something to say but could hardly get a word in.

Nicola was incensed. 'What's *he* doing here? I wasn't in his story!'

Charlotte sided with her, and Danny (Brian's friend) sided with him.

Eventually, Brian opened his clarinet case. 'Anyway, look what *we've* found!' He took out an old brown purse and handed it to the Writer.

'Got your address in it,' said Danny.

The Writer gasped. 'Oh, *no*!'

'What is it?'

'Mum's old purse.'

'Let's see!'

'Where'd you find it?'

'Woof!'

'Quit shovin'!'

'On the waste ground!'

'Let's *see*!'

'Back of Gimson's!'

'Woof!'

In this situation, if anything useful was to be achieved, somebody needed to take charge. Somebody did.

Nicola placed a hand on the Writer's shoulder and sought to console him. 'Charlotte, give him a chewie.'

'What flavour?' said Charlotte. 'Lemon – kiwi fruit –'

'Give him one.'

While the Writer exercised his jaw and calmed his nerves, Nicola set out her plan of campaign. He, the Writer, would stay where he was in case of further messages, or the Mysterious Men checking up on him. She and Charlotte would go down to the waste ground to search for clues.

'What about us?' cried Danny. 'Four's better than two.'

'Woof, woof!'

'And five's better than four!' yelled Brian. 'Timmy could follow the trail.'

Nicola considered this for a moment, raised her eyebrows to Charlotte and conceded the point.

So it was that at 4.15 on a
cooling May afternoon and
under an increasingly
peculiar sky, Nicola and
Charlotte, Brian, Danny
and Timmy set off for the
waste ground at the back
of Gimson's Shoe Factory
in the highest hopes of rescuing
the Writer's Mother. And Charlotte said,
'If we solve this, y'know . . . we could be famous.'

9

Five Following Clues

CHAOS now in Snuggleton-on-Sea. A velvet darkness cloaks the town; an eclipse, perhaps, though unpredicted by the weather men. A total power failure, the collapse of all phone lines and a holiday for the entire police force (the result, it seems, of a computer error) only add to the confusion. What's worse, two years apparently have passed since yesterday. Entire buildings have shot up or been demolished; new traffic lights have been installed – pedestrian precincts – one-way streets! As matches flare and candles flicker, couples who barely knew each other a few short hours ago now gaze in wonderment at 'wives' and 'husbands', three-piece suites, joint bank accounts and babies. The vicarage is crammed with kittens. Beards have sprouted; pimples too.

Meanwhile, the following items have gone missing:
    1   Fax machine from the Mayor's office
    1   Hot-air blower from the Moon and Sixpence Café
    3   Security lights from the back of Beatty's Supermarket

1   Wickerwork basket full of shoulder pads and helmets from the Snuggleton Sharks American Football Club

1   Pekinese from the Plumber (again)

9   New or reconditioned Hoovers from Currys Electrical Shop in the High Street

8   Medium deep-pan pizzas with extra toppings, 3 garlic breads, 6 regular Cokes, 2 Diet Cokes, 1 Vimto and the till from the Pizza Cabin

It was half-past five on a pitch-black May afternoon. Nicola and the others were approaching the waste ground at the back of Gimson's Shoe Factory.

'Which way now?' said Charlotte, puffing with her rucksack load of lemonade and buns.

'Left,' said Nicola.

They began to follow a narrow path. The darkness pressed in around them, unnaturally, like a black fog.

'Where did you find the purse?' said Nicola.

'Hard to say.' Brian shone his torch around.

Nicola held the purse out under Timmy's nose. The dog leapt joyfully on his lead, which didn't necessarily mean much. He grabbed the purse, shook it, dropped it and bounded off.

Meanwhile, the list of Snuggleton's missing items was growing:

1   Set of ladders from the Window Cleaner's
    yard
6   Cases of Pedigree Chum from the
    Cash'n'Carry
80 Pairs of ballet shoes from the La Calinda
    Dancing Academy
    The entire stock of cheese and pickled onion
    sandwiches from Stanley's Sandwich Bar on
    the promenade
14 Pianos from all over the place

It was some time later. The children were sitting on a
wall eating buns and drinking lemonade, with Timmy stretched out at their feet. In the past half hour
he had led the way in and out of various gardens, up
and over various fences, round and round any number
of lamp-posts, trees and bus shelters, but discovered
nothing.

Danny, despite the comfort of his cheese and . . . er,
coleslaw bun, was disappointed. 'This is hopeless.'

'No, it's not.' Nicola stood up.

'Well *I* think it's quite an adventure
already,' said Charlotte.

Brian directed his torch at the nearby
tennis pavilion. A line of confused
pigeons cooed nervously on the roof.
This and the heavy swell of the sea were
the only sounds to be heard.

what made
me say *that*?

Suddenly, Nicola yelled. 'Look there – a light!'

A curious phosphorescent glow was coming from the otherwise solid blackness of the Amusement Arcade. The children gathered up their things and crept forward. Brian and Nicola collided. 'Sh!' said Charlotte.

The doors to the Arcade were open. In the torchlight Nicola and the others could make out the ranks of computer games, pinball and fruit machines. Farther off, however, there was . . . something else; something else which hovered in mid-air and shone: a single silver hand.

The children fell back in disarray.

Then: 'I know what it is!' cried Charlotte. 'It's the Palmist.'

And so it was: The Electronic Palmist, a somewhat old-fashioned machine which for 20p would read your palm and tell your fortune.

'See, you're supposed to put your hand on the glass like this.' Charlotte demonstrated. 'Put your money in – and a card comes out.'

'Yes, but what's it doing on at all?' said Brian.

'Independent power supply,' suggested Danny.

'Yes, but why?'

Nicola stepped up to the machine, took out a coin and dropped it in the slot. An immediate whirring noise, a burst of music. Briefly the light from the hand flickered and throbbed. A card popped out.

'What's it say?'
'Shine your torch.'
'Read it!'
Nicola read:

> *For the knowledge you are seeking*
> *For the lady you would find*
> *See the stone man in the market*
> *He has something on his mind.*

Meanwhile . . . half a dozen hymn-books and a radio from the Vicar's Vauxhall Viva, one seagoing barge from the harbour and – oh, no! – a *cake* from Clifford Avenue.

The children stood in the market place gasping for breath and staring up at the life-size statue of Sir Frobisher Pitt-Jones: his splendid horse, mighty forearm, steadfast gaze, and . . .

'Look – on his hat!'
'Something white!'
'Another clue, I'll bet!'
'Climb up!'

Another clue it was, stuck to Sir Frobisher's hat with Blu-Tack. Danny, the climber, read it out:

> *'On the trail of someone's mother*
> *If you need another sign*
> *Read a garage door in Dove Street*
> *Painted orange – number nine.'*

Off they went again, with pounding hearts and bouncing rucksacks.

After Dove Street they followed the trail to the fire station, and from there to Snuggleton Dairies, and from there . . . The clues they encountered were varied and ingenious. One was written on a dirty windscreen; another on a balloon, unreadable until inflated. One was buried.

Eventually, however, the children became suspicious. These clues *were* clues, it seemed, but only to other clues. The trail was endless or, failing that, circular. This last idea occurred to them when, two hours later, they arrived once more in the vicinity of the tennis pavilion.

'Is there anyone for tennis?
Step on court and don't despair
Read the message in the moonlight
Underneath the umpire's chair.'

But the children did no such thing.

'Blow the umpire's chair!' they cried and slumped along the wall.

'I give up.'

'Me too.'

'Anyway, what moonlight?'

Whereupon, right on cue, a pale moon with a scatter of glittering stars appeared in the sky above the pavilion. The unnatural fog-like darkness had gone; natural night was taking its place.

'Ah!' (for relief).

'Oh!' (in amazement) the children gasped.

'Coo!' cooed the pigeons.

Next thing: *footsteps.*

'Look out!'

'Gerroverthewall!'

Over they went, then crouched and peered back. A cloud had passed across the moon, dimming its light. In the distance something was moving.

Presently, a straggling line of Mysterious Men came strolling along the promenade. One was pushing a remarkably full Marks and Spencer's trolley; another had a school crossing sign over his shoulder; two others were carrying a rolled-up carpet.

With jangling nerves, the children observed the procession as it went by. They saw, or thought they saw, the rolled-up carpet . . . wriggling.

10

Mysterious Men

HOUSE BY HOUSE and street by street the lights are coming on in Snuggleton-on-Sea, phones are ringing and the soon-to-be-baffled police are beginning to report for duty. On Quarry Hill, the Mysterious Men observe the tide of light which is heading their way, but seem unconcerned. The tall one lifts the little one up to get a better view. The fat one whistles.

The Mysterious Men move on with clattering trolley across the dark uneven ground. For a moment their silhouettes stand out against the moonlit sky. A sudden burp and burst of laughter fill the air. The moon goes in behind a cloud. When it returns, flooding the hill with silver light, the men are no-where to be seen.

The disappearance was complete and the children saw it. They had been trailing the men for twenty minutes.

'Did y'see that?' cried Charlotte. 'How could they –'

'Sh!' said Nicola.

Far off, yet maybe not so far, an echoing voice –

'Heigh ho, heigh ho!' – and accompanying ghostly whistle.

'Grr!' growled Timmy.

Cautiously the children advanced across the bumpy grass. The moon was in again behind the clouds. They could see . . . not a lot. Then: a screwed-up ball of fish-and-chip paper, a shopping trolley (empty) and a big black hole with a window cleaner's ladder leading . . . down.

The hole was like a chimney in the earth or a dry well. Getting Timmy down the ladder was the tricky bit. At the bottom, leaves, crisp bags and a dozy frog. Also a tunnel.

'Look!' cried Nicola.

A faint light glimmered.

'Listen!'

Distant hollow footsteps.

'Come on!'

The tunnel sloped downwards, straight at first then twisting. Its roof was low in places. Elsewhere their rucksacks scraped the sides. Water trickled on their heads and once they had to step across a rushing stream.

The children were becoming apprehensive.

'How much further?'

'I don't like it here.'

'My torch is packin' up.'

Nicola slipped off her rucksack and sat on it. The others followed suit. 'Come on,' she said. 'Don't give up now. We must be . . .'

Up ahead there was a small sound like a tinkling piano, and a smell too – frying bacon! Then there

was a noise *behind* them: something dragging . . . rasping breath.

'Oooh!' cried Danny.

A harsh light lit up the tunnel. Caught in its glare, the children could see little; just a looming shape, a pair of eyes and the glittering barrel of a gun.

'An . . . *zup*!'

Following their shadows, urged on by grunts from the mysterious gunman, Nicola and the others continued down the tunnel. (Timmy, though, you will

71

observe, did not.) Eventually, after much stumbling –

'Gerrup!'

and attempts at whispered conversation –

'Shurrup!'

they found themselves at the entrance to an enormous cave. It contained, well, fourteen pianos for a start, one of which the fat Mysterious Man was playing. There were crates and barrels and cardboard boxes; bicycles, ballet shoes, ladders, birds in cages and a cement mixer. There were a couple of wardrobes, four beds, three hammocks, an ornamental fountain and a substantial quantity of garden furniture. There was a portable stove, two catering-size frying pans and a kitchen table loaded with eggs, bacon, mushrooms, sausage, black pudding and beans. There was a mountain of mailbags, a library of books, five portraits in oil of past mayors of the town and a selection of policemen's truncheons. There was an orange tree in a brass pot.

The cave was lit by Calor gas lamps and a couple of security lights lashed to ladders. Even so, the greater part of that colossal space was lost in darkness.

As the children crossed the threshold, the man behind them bellowed, 'Har!'

A piano lid clunked, beer bottles clinked, a frying pan clanged, and a number of other Mysterious Men emerged from the shadows.

The children huddled together.

Charlotte whispered, 'Where's Timmy g–'

'Sh!' said Nicola.

The Mysterious Men were in a huddle too, and muttering.

'Woot!'

'Werf!'

'Warra warra warrarat!' it sounded like.

Presently, the tallest of them attempted to translate himself into halfway intelligible English. 'What you lot doin' 'ere?'

The children were dismayed and scared, of course, but defiant too.

'Mind your own business!' cried Nicola.

'Yes,' said Brian. 'You don't own this cave, y'know.'

'Maybe not,' growled the tall man. 'We own this wardrobe, though.' He gestured behind him. 'Any more lip and you'll be in it.'

Even then Nicola refused to be silenced. 'What have you done with the Writer's Mother?'

For a moment the men were taken aback.

'You ought to be ashamed of yourselves!'

'Yeah?' cried the littlest man. 'Well, we ain't.'

Which was the truth. They weren't ashamed at all; they were proud. So proud that soon they were boasting – and interrupting each other to do so – about the cleverness of their crimes and the ingenuity of their hideout. No doubt they would have continued for some time if Brian, in exasperation, hadn't yelled: 'You'll be sorry when the *police* get here!'

That stopped them.

'What police?'

'Gerroff!'

'He's bluffin'.'

'No, he's not,' said Nicola. 'See this?' She held out Timmy's lead. 'A dog's lead.'

'Yeah?'

'Worrovit?'

'Well,' said Nicola, smiling, ' . . . no dog.'

No dog. The Mysterious Men understood the significance of this at once.

'Where is he then?'

They looked about them. The fat one took a step or two towards the tunnel.

'It's no use looking,' said Nicola. 'He's gone – for help.'

Now it was the children's turn to boast – of Timmy's prowess. He'd fetch the police all right, and like a shot! He was the smartest dog in Snuggleton!

The Mysterious Men appeared
confused. They frowned and made
jokes about Lassie. Meanwhile,
another dog – the Plumber's Pekinese – was showing
his prowess by releasing himself from the rolled-up
carpet.

A phone rang. It was a mobile one in the tall man's
jacket pocket. He took it out. 'Yeah . . . Nar . . . Nar
. . . Warrat? . . . Woot . . . WOOT?'

The news, it seemed, was not good. The tall man
hurled his phone to the floor and jumped on it.

The Mysterious Men were worried. While the one
with the gun stood guard, the others muttered and
dashed about.

Danny and Brian exchanged glances.

'Will Timmy really . . . er, y'know?'

'Yes – bound to . . . I hope.'

The men were assembling
now, carrying things:
mailbag – suitcase – Pizza
Cabin till. The fat one walked
over to a wardrobe, unlocked it
and growled inside. Blinking and
staggering slightly, out stepped
the Writer's Mother.

'Ah!' Nicola and the others
rushed forward.

I think he wants us to follow him!

'Gar!'

'My word,' exclaimed the Writer's Mother. 'It's Betsy Brown!'

'No – Nicola.'

'Woot!'

'Ah, yes. I was forgetting.'

'We've come to rescue you,' said Brian.

'It's very good of you,' the Writer's Mother said.

'Warrawarrarat!'

And now there was a definite sense of urgency. They were leaving the cave along a different, broader tunnel: Mysterious Men front and rear, children and Writer's Mother in between. The tunnel sloped downwards. A dull, ponderous noise was sounding up ahead.

Nicola said, 'I think we're –'

'Shurrup!' growled the nearest Mysterious Man.

The noise grew louder, heavier, wilder, so that the tunnel itself appeared to throb.

Nicola said, 'I th-'

'Rup!' growled the man.

A breeze, a wind, a *gale* began to blow. There was a familiar powerful smell, a tremendous crash of water and –

'The sea!' cried Nicola. 'Told you.'

The children and the Writer's Mother stood on the beach. A violent barrage of air was slanting over them. It sucked the breath right out of their mouths. They were instantly soaked by spray and rain. Huge cliffs loomed up behind them. There was a jetty and a great black ship.

The Mysterious Men, meanwhile, were off, scrambling over the sand, clambering up the jetty steps, mounting the gang-plank.

'They're gettin' away!' yelled Brian.

Engines throbbed, chains rattled. A powerful light from the ship's stern illuminated the shore. The ship was pulling off; a ragged cheer from the men, dismay on the beach. Then out of the tunnel and into the swinging beam of light stepped the Pekinese.

'Yap!'

The wind caught him, bowled him over and blew him along like a lost hat.

The Writer's Mother was first to react. Rushing forward, she snatched the Pekinese from the raging water's edge, lost her footing – 'Help!' – and was submerged.

Nicola was there, with Brian, Charlotte, Danny.

'Hold hands!' she cried. 'Make a chain!'

'Help!'

'Yap, yap!'

'Hold on!'

Blinded by spray, deafened by pounding waves, the children struggled at their hopeless task. Knee deep they were, waist deep, coughing and spluttering, fearing for themselves. Charlotte lost *her* footing then and screamed.

Nicola was under water – upside-down, it felt like – thrashing around and choking; a terrible tightness in her chest.

Then, suddenly, when all seemed lost, the rescuers were rescued; plucked from that violent sea by sturdy and determined arms and carried safe to shore.

Nicola lay on her back and opened her eyes. Breathing hard from their exertions, *the Mysterious Men were all around her*!

She attempted to speak. 'But why . . .?'

The men just shook their heads and shrugged.

'Who knows?'

'Beats me.'

'Can't think what came over us!' . . . it sounded like.

Nicola's eyelids fluttered.

Moments later, the police came scrambling down onto the beach with Timmy leading the way. They found the children and

the Writer's Mother soaked but safe enough. The jetty was deserted.

Out in the bay, a great black ship was butting off into the surging sea. Patches of yellow light glowed in the wheelhouse; shapes moved. Then curtains of rain and darkness came down around it, and the ship was gone.

11

The End

MIDNIGHT: Snuggleton police station, blankets and hot drinks all round, anxious parents summoned.

The Writer's Mother was full of praise for the children; so were the police. Later, Nicola heard the Sergeant telling her dad they were, 'the pluckiest kids he'd ever come upon', and Timmy was the smartest dog. Which reminds me: dog biscuits and Pedigree Chum all round.

Nicola in her blanket and her mother's arms was falling asleep (the other three had fallen). The lights, phones and scurrying feet of the station were fading away. She heard – half-heard – the police again . . . more questions.

'Concerning these Mysterious Men, sir.'

'Ah, yes.' (Was that the Writer?)

'We understand you may be able to help us.'

'Not really.' (It was!) 'The truth is, they're a bit of a mystery to *me*.'

It was half-past two on a bright May afternoon and the Writer in his shed was joyful.

'The End!'

He pushed his chair back from the desk and looked out of the window. The sky was a pale and sparkling blue. A haze of midges hovered in the air above the lupins. The neighbour's cat came strolling up the path.

The Writer yawned. He rearranged his desk and made a cup of tea. He sat in the easy chair with a couple of holiday brochures. He dozed off.

Bang! The door flew open and a small muscular boy came hurtling in. He stared fiercely about him, declared, 'There's none toys in here!', and hurtled out.

The Writer leapt to his feet. Mr and Mrs Brown were in the doorway.

'It's all right,' said Mrs Brown wearily. 'We've promised to take him to Toys 'Я' Us.'

The Writer frowned. 'Yes, but who is he?'

'You should ask,' said Mrs Brown.

'It's the *baby*,' added Mr Brown. 'Two years on.'

'Ah yes – the baby!' the Writer slapped his forehead. 'Forgot him again.'

The little boy – William by name – burst back in.

'Hey!' The Writer was alarmed.

William (Billy most of the time) grabbed some pages and scrunched them in his chubby fist.

'*Hey!*'

'He's into everything,' said Mrs Brown. 'Bernard, do something.'

Mr Brown held out his hand – 'Come and see the rabbits' – and lured Billy away.

Mrs Brown sat on the swivel chair. 'We need to talk.'

'Oh, yes?'

'About this two-years-later-business.'

'Ah!' The Writer was smoothing out his pages.

'It won't do.'

'Why not? I thought –'

'You *thought*? That's the trouble, you don't think. Young children out till all hours – Mysterious Men – half drowned!'

'Well . . .'

'Even your own mother – kidnapped – just for a good story.'

The Writer, who had been looking downcast, perked

up. 'Hm – wasn't bad, was it?'

Mrs Brown sighed. 'That's not the point. Anyway, now Brian's saying *he* wants to be *sixteen*. They're wishing our lives away.' She took out a tissue and blew her nose. 'So that's it. We want things back *just as they were.*'

'I see. What does Betsy – er, Nicola – say?'

'She won't hear of it.'

'Ah.' The Writer thought for a moment. 'The thing is, I've finished.' He indicated his smoothed-out pages. 'See: "The End".'

Mrs Brown was unconvinced. 'That's no problem – start again.'

There was a thump at the side of the shed; Billy was back. His little face peeped round the door.

'Four stories,' said the Writer, 'one each, that's what we said.'

Mr Brown rejoined them. 'A story each, did you say?'

'That's right.'

'You've missed one then.' Mr Brown smiled ruefully. 'He wants his.'

'Oh, yes, I forgot about that.' Mrs Brown drew Billy towards her and stroked his hair. 'Tell the man what you want.'

Billy then was struck by shyness. 'Wantastory,' he muttered gruffly.

The Writer seemed nonplussed.

'Tell him what sort of story,' said Mr Brown.
'Wanta Chrissmus story.'
'What?'
' . . . Chrissmus story.'

'Christmas?' The Writer frowned. '*Christmas* – it's only May!'

Billy raised his head, bolder again. 'I *want* one.'

The Browns departed. The Writer sat at his desk contemplating the view, sipping cold tea. He put the holiday brochures away in a drawer. He stared as though in a trance at the blank page in front of him. He began to write.

Meanwhile, down on Sibson Road Mr and Mrs Brown with Billy between them were heading for home. Mrs Brown was shivering in her short-sleeved frock. A chill breeze had begun to blow. Grey clouds were moving across the sky. The leaves were falling.

12

Different Snow

A STONISHMENT once more in Snuggleton-on-Sea. Time is flying; there is a great acceleration in the seasons, a vast fast-forwarding of weather. Sun shining – fruit ripening – leaves falling – swallows departing – gales blowing – councils gritting – trees bare – birds hungry . . . snow.

It was four o'clock on this unexpected Christmas Eve. The bewildered Runner (with blue knees) was returning from a twenty-kilometre circuit of the town, begun in early summer. The Plumber was searching for his low-slung little dog in the back (snow-drifted) garden. A number of office parties were in full swing.

Elsewhere, the town was a frantic scrum of extra-late last-minute shoppers. The loaded Postman staggered through the streets. Sudden turkeys were heading for the oven, puddings for the pot. Decorations, hastily acquired, were being hastily hung. Lighted trees now glowed in many of the windows.

Meanwhile, in Clifford Avenue . . .

Billy Brown was busy in the garden. He rolled a ball of snow. When he could roll it no further, he began to roll another. When this became too big, he got his brother to place one on top of the other. He got his sister to fetch a chair from the kitchen. A third ball was raised up on the other two and a fourth and smaller one piled on top. Billy shovelled snow with his plastic spade and patted it in place with gloved

hands. He obtained certain items of clothing and a small orange. He got some little bits of coal.

Billy stood in the garden. From the dark sky in the still air, large flakes were drifting down. His breath was white in front of him, his gloves soaking wet. The *Snowman* was complete.

Bathtime: steam and bubbles, toothpaste and pyjamas. Bedtime story – kisses – Christmas stocking – shadows on the bedroom wall – peeping at the Snowman down below. Voices in the hallway . . . fading. Teddy, thumb and sleep.

Billy was out of bed. The house was quiet. He slipped his slippers on and dressing-gown and hurried to the window. The snow had ceased, the sky was clear, a glittering light was bouncing from the frost-bound garden – and the Snowman raised his hat.

Billy went down to let him in. The Snowman, however, had other ideas. He wanted Billy to come out.

'Spozed to come in first,' said Billy, gruffly. 'Play in my room – scare the cat – try my dad's trousers on.'

'No.' The Snowman shook his head, producing a little shower of snow. 'Don't like 'ouses. Now, igloos, that's different.'

'Spozed to cool yourself in the freezer,' continued Billy. 'Ride the motorbike.'

The Snowman looked around. 'What motorbike?'

'Well . . .' Billy stepped into the garden.

'Also,' said the Snowman, smiling, 'what cat?'

Billy was confused.

'See,' the Snowman took Billy's hand and strolled

into the street with him, 'what you're thinkin' is, I'm *The Snowman*, ain't ya?'

Billy nodded.

'Like in the video and all that.'

'Hm,' said Billy.

'Well, the thing is – I ain't.' The Snowman rubbed his chin (more snow). 'I'm the other Snowman.'

'Oh!' said Billy.

'Yeah.' The Snowman paused beneath a street lamp. 'See: different 'at and scarf, different coal and orange; and' – he blew a tiny blizzard from his upraised hand – '*entirely* different snow.'

On they strolled through the sleeping town. Billy was silent, unsure what to expect. They approached the children's playground on Totters Lane.

''Ere, swings!' cried the Snowman. 'Come on!'

Billy sat on a swing while the Snowman pushed. The Snowman sat on the swing while Billy pushed.

'Wheee!' the Snowman cried. 'I'm flyin'!'

Billy stopped pushing. A frown appeared on his smooth little face. 'Flying,' he said. Then, 'You're spozed to *really* fly.'

'What?'

'That's the best bit.'

But the Snowman disagreed. 'Not for me, it ain't. No 'ead for 'eights. Did y'ever see that film *Vertigo*?'

'No,' said Billy. 'Spozed to fly to the North Pole.'

'North Pole? That's miles away.'

'Spozed to.' Billy sat dejectedly on a snowy bench. Across the park, beyond the frozen lake, a duck quacked loudly in the darkness.

The Snowman got up from his swing. 'Come on, then – give us your 'and.'

Billy and the Snowman ran across the grass: fast – faster – as fast as ever they could. For a moment they were skimming along like pebbles on a pond. And then they flew.

The flight was everything that Billy could have hoped for: a swooping, soaring trip across the town, with frosty stars above and rolling sea beyond. Tiny houses – shrouded trees – glittering street lights –

scribbly tracks in the snow – bobbing boats in the
harbour – a miniature man on Quarry Hill walking
his miniature dog.

Billy saw it all and was bewitched. The Snowman
saw none of it. ''Ad me eyes shut!' he exclaimed as
they landed (in the Vicar's garden, actually). He
looked around. 'I could do with a smoke.'

As it happened, there was another Snowman
standing nearby, rather smart, with top hat and pipe.

'May I?'

'Be my guest, old chap,' the Vicar's Snowman said.

'Ta!' The Snowman took a puff.

Billy watched in silence. When they were out in the street, he said, 'Which Snowman was he?'

'He was . . . the Third Snowman,' said the Snowman. 'Come on – bedtime.'

Meanwhile, back at Number 38 Billy's dad was dreaming. He dreamt his little boy was flying with a snowman. 'Seems somewhat unlikely,' he informed his wife (in his dream).

'Never mind unlikely,' Billy's mum declared. 'It's dangerous.'

That morning Billy was the first to wake. He sat in bed in a frenzy of joy and opened his presents. Outside, the garden gradually emerged from darkness. Snow was falling again. Billy stood at the window and stared out. The Snowman was still there, his simple body planted on the ground, his simple face gazing.

It had a pipe in it . . . of course.

13

The Thing Is

HERE WE STILL ARE in the peaceful and popular little – well, I believe you know all that. Things, of course, have changed a great deal since – but, there again, you know all *that*.

Hm . . .

Now it is Boxing Day, a time to relax and let the turkey go down, play with presents. A time also for cliff-top walks – charity football matches – visiting friends. The Mayor and his family, for instance, are visiting the Vicar and his family: admiring, in fact, his fine top-hatted Snowman at this very moment. The Café Owner (divorced) is calling on his ex-wife to collect his little daughter and take her sledging up on Quarry Hill. Gerry the Milkman is visiting his favourite pub, The Baskerville Hound, for a lunch-time glass of shandy.

Meanwhile, our old friends the Browns are on their way to call upon . . . a man they know in Slope Street.

The Writer and his mother were pleased to see them. Presents were exchanged, and mince pies and mulled wine consumed. By and by the Writer's Mother led Billy away to see the rabbits. Mrs Brown took the opportunity to speak.

'We've been thinking again, about this two-year business.'

The Writer nodded and sipped his wine.

'The thing is . . . we'd like the baby back.'

'We'd like the puppy back as well,' said Brian.

'We've missed him growing up, you see,' said Mrs

Brown. 'It's all been . . . such a rush.'

'Hm.' The Writer rubbed his chin.

Through the window Billy could be seen moving purposefully round the garden. He was rolling a ball of snow.

The Writer frowned. 'Better stop him, I think. He'll want his story again.'

Mr Brown went out. In his absence, the others raised the subject of things they *didn't* want back: Mrs Brown's unwavy hair, Nicola's old name, Bernard's boring bank job.

Wait and see!

It sounded like

'Yes, Dad's job,' said Nicola firmly. 'When we asked you before, you said you were working on it.'

'I am,' the Writer said (actually, he'd forgotten). 'I *have*, er . . . look in the paper tomorrow; small ads.'

'What sort of job?' said Mrs Brown.

'Will he like it?' the children cried.

'Will he *get* it?'

But the Writer, with a mouthful of mince pie, merely shrugged and mumbled. 'Wait and see,' it sounded like.

It was three o'clock on a clear December (?) afternoon in Snuggleton-on-Sea. The Browns were homeward bound on Sibson Road. A peculiar feeling gripped them all, a fleeting sense of living in reverse, memories of the future . . . fading. They carried coats and scarves; the temperature was rising, a terrific thaw had gripped the town. At their heels ran Timmy, whose head had somehow slipped his collar, whose solid bark was modulating to a puppy's yap. While smiling Mrs Brown had frowning *baby* Billy curled up in her arms.

THE END